A day O at the Animal Post Office

Sharon Rentta

Jack is sending
an email to his best friend, Polly.
Polly has gone to live at the North Pole,
which is a seriously long way away.

Jack really misses her.

Jack's dad says he should send Polly a letter. Dad's a postman himself, so he knows all about letters, and how they travel all around the world.

Jack thinks that's a brilliant idea. He's going to need his best paints and felt pens for this.

Craft
+ paint
Stuff

First he paints Polly a
totally fantastic picture.

Then he writes her an
utterly amazing letter.
It takes a lot of thinking.

Dear Polly,
I miss you,
love Jack
xxx

He stuffs it in an envelope and writes Polly's
address on it nice and clearly.

Then he licks the
glue to make it stick.
It tastes pretty nasty.

He just needs a stamp now, and that means a trip to the Post Office.
It's hard to make dads run fast enough, even when
there are urgent letters to send.

There's often a bit of a queue at the Post Office.

In the Post Office, Dad waits in the queue while Jack checks
out what's going on. People are sending letters and parcels, buying
birthday cards and even having their photo taken in the Photo Booth.

People aren't always that happy if you
sneak into the Photo Booth with them.

These are some of the things you can't put in the post:

Ice cubes,
because they'll melt.

Eggs,
in case
they break.

Goldfish,
because their
water would
spill.

A cactus,
because it's
too prickly.

This dog is posting a bone.
It's important to wrap it up well,
so it doesn't get broken.

Pop!

Pop!

The best thing about bubble wrap
is popping the bubbles.

Post is weighed to see how many stamps it needs. Jack's letter is going to cost quite a lot, because it's got to travel over two thousand miles.

Jack sits on the scales to see how much it would cost to post himself. He'd be quite pricey.

Now the letter goes into the postbox – and it's on its way to Polly!

It's going to take a few days to get there, so Dad tells Jack all about what happens next.

First, one of Dad's postal-worker friends
collects Jack's letter from the postbox.
Her name is Hattie, and her job is to
collect all of the letters from all
of the postboxes all over town.

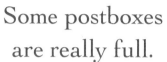
Some postboxes
are really full.

And sometimes there's a surprise inside.
This rat fell into the postbox while
posting his letter. He's very grateful
when Hattie lets him out.

Hattie tips the post into
big sacks and heaves
them into her van.

These are some of the letters Hattie's
collected today:

a birthday card
for one of Jack's
schoolfriends,

a card from a mouse
to his granny to
say "Thank you
for my new
scarf",

an invitation to a party,

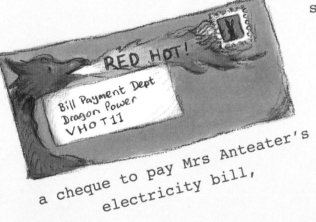

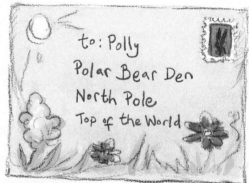

a cheque to pay Mrs Anteater's
electricity bill,

and Jack's letter to Polly.

It's hard work lifting all those
mail sacks. Hattie needs a tea
break, before she drives the
letters to the Sorting Office.

The Sorting Office is full of whizzy machinery, which reads the addresses on the envelopes, and sorts the letters into boxes. There are boxes for all the different towns and countries.

Thousands of letters are sorted every night.

It's a good job for owls, as they like staying awake all night.

"Is mine the only letter going to the North Pole?" asks Jack. "No," says Dad. "There are loads for Father Christmas, as well."

Once the post has been sorted, it's time for it to go on its way. Forklift trucks are handy for loading crates of letters into lorries. It's a good idea to let go of the crate before it's hoisted into the air.

The letters are loaded into vans . . .

. . . and on to trains, so they can travel all over the country.

"Is my letter
on a train?" asks Jack.
"No," says Dad. "Your letter
has to travel by . . .

"Aeroplane!"

The plane flies through the night, over
the sea and the ice, thousands
of miles, all the way to . . .

. . . the North Pole.

The North Pole Sorting Office
is a great big igloo. It's pretty chilly inside,
but everyone keeps warm by lugging parcels around.

The Sorting Office gives each postie a
sack of mail to deliver.

The best way to travel round the
North Pole is on skis, or by quad bike.

Walruses are good at delivering the post in the Arctic. They're not that quick, but they don't feel the cold. This walrus has a very important task . . .

. . . she's just delivered Jack's letter to Polly!
Polly reads it – then she dashes inside her igloo to write a letter back to Jack.

It's over a week since Jack sent his letter. He's excited today, because Dad has said he can give him a hand at work.

Here they are down at the Sorting Office. Dad's got a sackful of letters to deliver to all the people in their town, and Jack's going to help him.

The postmen and postwomen start work really early in the morning. A cup of coffee and a biscuit helps perk them up before they set out on their rounds.

Oi! This letter
isn't mine!

Monkeys are quick,
but a bit slap-dash.

Giraffes are good at delivering
post to high-up houses.

boing!

Kangaroos don't need a mail sack.
They just use their pouches.

Jack's dad has a bicycle, which is just as
well when there's this much post to deliver.

Jack has his own special way of sorting the letters.

At last they're on their way. They cycle all around town,
stopping at every house to deliver the post.

They deliver gas bills,

postcards,

and even magazines. Soon, there's just one letter left.
"Why are you posting it through **our** front door?" asks Jack.

"Because it's for you!" says Dad.
Jack dashes inside and tears
open the envelope.

It's from Polly! She's sent him a letter, all the way from the North Pole, and it says she's coming to visit!

It's not easy waiting for Polly to arrive, but Jack has to be patient. The days definitely go by faster if he does a lot of bouncing.

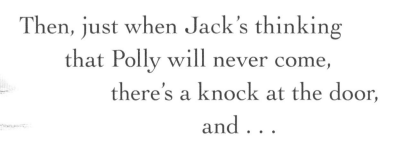

Then, just when Jack's thinking that Polly will never come, there's a knock at the door, and . . .

. . . Polly's here!

And she's just in
time for tea.

For my mum, who writes lovely letters.

First published in 2016 by Alison Green Books
An imprint of Scholastic Children's Books
Euston House, 24 Eversholt Street, London NW1 1DB
A division of Scholastic Ltd
www.scholastic.co.uk
London – New York – Toronto – Sydney – Auckland
Mexico City – New Delhi – Hong Kong

HB ISBN: 978 1407162 28 7
PB ISBN: 978 1407162 54 6